One Arabian Morning

By Pete Marlowe + Illustrated by Charles Bell

ANNICK PRESS

TORONTO + NEW YORK + VANCOUVER

Katelyn had a notepad,
 and she had a pencil behind her ear.

"Cold cereal for me," said her father.

 Katelyn wrote that down.

"You'll have to get up awfully early," said her mother.

"I'm setting my own alarm clock," said Katelyn.

"Then I'll have cereal as well," said her mother. "And a big pot of tea."

Katelyn wrote that down too. She set her own alarm clock.
She kissed her mother and father good night. "Make sure you get
right off to sleep," said her mother.

But Katelyn knew she'd never get to sleep.
She lay awake forever. She was too excited
about making her parents breakfast
in bed and all the adventures
morning would —

BRRINGGG!

Katelyn's head jumped off the
pillow. Katelyn's hand jumped from the
blankets and hit the alarm clock.
And the alarm clock jumped off
the bedside table and fell with
a ringing and bounced with a buzzing
and Katelyn jumped half out of bed and
fell half on the floor, and her hands
looked for the ringing all over the dark,
and then the room rang quiet.

Katelyn pushed herself back up into bed.
"I don't have to get up right away,"
she said. "I can just lie back in bed for
a minute or so."

Katelyn had never been so wide awake. She closed her eyes, and
the sound of the alarm clock ringing and then falling still echoed
and bounced around in her head, and behind all that buzzing
was a smaller buzzing, from way behind her right ear, and Katelyn
tried to find her way out of the big buzzing and back to the quieter
buzzing behind.

"It sort of sounds like someone's voice," thought Katelyn. "I wonder
what they're talking about. I bet if I got just a bit closer. Yes.
It's definitely a voice now, but I still can't tell what they're saying.
I'll have to go closer."

Now Katelyn was walking down a dark hallway, with light coming through the doorway at the end. She followed the murmur of the voice.

"Murmur murmur my king, and if you don't bumble rumble all the treasure will be scrumble and burmur."

Katelyn stopped at the big door and peeked through the keyhole. She saw fancy carpets on the floor and candles along the walls, and she saw a throne, with a very worried man in it, holding a scepter and wearing a robe, and from the top of his head shone a crown.

Katelyn pushed the door open a crack now, and saw people, lots of people —

    courtiers and merchants and princes and barbers

    jewelry sellers and jewelry buyers

    a princess, a sailor

    a minaret crier

    people with fezzes and people with turbans

    people with swords and sharp old-fashioned weapons

    people who looked like they rode in on stallions and

    people who looked like bare camelback riders —

all of them listening, listening like Katelyn, to the mumble and murmur, and if Katelyn could just push the door just a little bit wider…

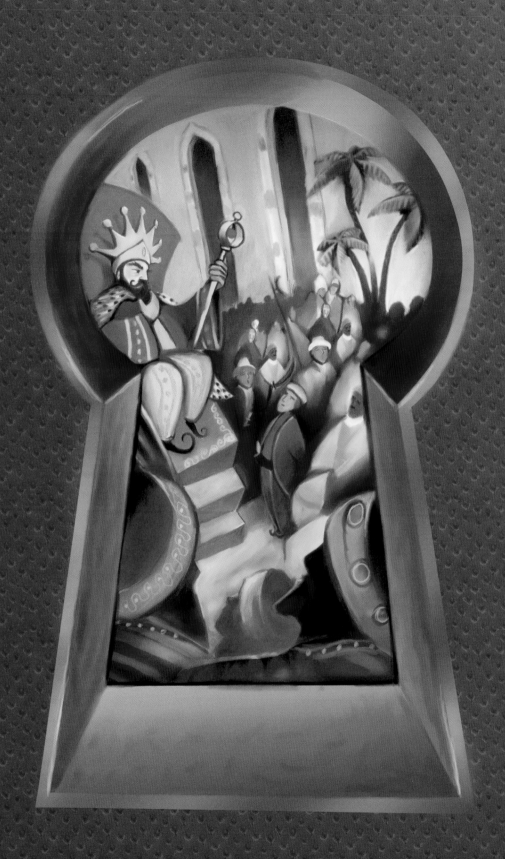

Then far across the king's chambers, by a treasure chest, a man was speaking, with the same mumble murmur Katelyn had followed all the way from her bed, and he held up her mom's teapot, high over his head.

"Maybe I can ask him for it back," said Katelyn. "Maybe I could say, 'If you'll excuse me, I'm the girl who heard you from my faraway bed in the long away future.'"

Katelyn stuck a tiptoe out around the door.

"Now I have the magic lamp," the man with the teapot cackled. "And now I am the Grand Vizier of all the kingdom. And the greatest treasure shall be mine."

The man with the cackle opened the teapot. And
Katelyn's tiptoe stretched out on slippery air and then
pulled the rest of her like a vacuum, all the way into
the dusty old teapot. Then the man squished the lid
down, and from inside Katelyn could hear his voice
in the dark.

"Muffle muffle my silly old kuffle," the voice spuffled.
"Now I have the powerful genie ruffled up in my muffle."

Katelyn felt a sneeze twisting and turning all the way
to the edge of her nose. She huffled and snuffled.
Her eyes misted and her arms twisted, for the pocket
of her pajamas and the handkerchief there.

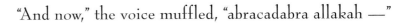

"And now," the voice muffled, "abracadabra allakah —"

CHHOOO!

And the lid sneezed off the teapot, and the handkerchief ruffled out on the floor, while Katelyn grew like a smoke storm, high up to the ceiling, and up through the rooftop and high through the sky, and all the way up past the clouds.

She pushed them out of her way.

And far down below, in the middle of the desert, she saw the tops of a town, with a palace in the middle, and in the middle of the palace she saw the legs of her pajamas, disappearing down through the roof.

She bent. Bent down through the clouds and bent down through the sky, down above the town and the towers of the palace, and down through the ceiling, and then down upon her hands and her knees.

"That's right. Bow down to me, slave," said a tiny little voice from a tiny little man with a tiny little teapot. "Because I am the Grand Vizier of all the kingdom, and for my first wish, I want all the king's court turned into stone."

Katelyn tried not to. She tried to hold back the wish
like holding back a sneeze, with the king's court all
running this way, and she held up her breath and
scrunched up her eyes, with the king's court all running
that way, and then she plugged up her nose.

But the abra was growing. The cadabra was buzzing.
And the allakah zoomed, past her holding and scrunching
and plugging, and all the king's court were frozen that
way and this way, except the Grand Vizier, who cackled.

"Now slave," the Grand Vizier said. "A thousand years ago
the first king of this realm took his greatest treasure,
and he locked it away in this chest. For my second wish,
I want this chest opened up, and the greatest treasure
in the kingdom will be mine."

Then all was dark. Until a line of light appeared, and grew to a crack and then to a flood, and Katelyn looked up from inside the treasure chest and saw the Grand Vizier, huge as the sky, looking down into the chest with a grin. And then the grin disappeared.

"There's nothing here," the Grand Vizier said. "The chest is empty."

"What do you mean, empty?" said Katelyn.

"What are you doing way down in there?" said the Grand Vizier. "What have you done with the most precious treasure in the kingdom?"

Katelyn jumped up onto the edge of the treasure chest.

"Maybe I am the most precious treasure in the kingdom,"
said Katelyn. "Did you ever think of that? And maybe
you haven't noticed what else is in there. If you peek
down in the very furthest bottomest corner, I think you'll
find what you're looking for."

"I don't see anything," said the Grand Vizier.

"Look closer."

"I still don't."

"Then closer."

"If I get any closer I'll have to climb right into the chest."

"Then I guess you don't want to bother," said Katelyn.

"Oh, all right," the Grand Vizier said, and he climbed
up onto the edge of the treasure chest, and crawled right
down in.

Then Katelyn did a handstand up on top
of the chest and pushed down with all the
pushing she could push with, and —

WHHUUMP!

The whump blew a whoosh all over the
king's chambers, and the frozen court
were all running again, out that door
and this door, and Katelyn was flipped
off the falling top of the treasure chest
and somersaulted onto her handkerchief
swirling on whooshes of wind, and
Katelyn said:

"I hope I don't hurt myself when I fall."

And the handkerchief wiffled beneath
her, this way, then that way, slowly
back down.

"I hope," said Katelyn, "I'll be able to find
a way to get home."

And the handkerchief flew. Up to the ceiling and down to the carpet, wherever Katelyn hoped it would go.

"Lup me oup," said a muffle from the treasure chest.

"I won't let you out," said Katelyn. "But I'll leave you a wish. Handkerchief, I hope you can pick up the teapot."

The handkerchief could, and the handkerchief did, and Katelyn scrambled up to the top of the teapot, and then rubbed it, and called:

"For your third wish, if you wish to become the most precious treasure in the kingdom, a girl from the furthest of time will come to find you."

Then Katelyn rode with her hopes out the window, out into the desert, and all the way home.

Of course she had to swoop down into the Nile River to fill up the teapot, then fly low over India to pick up some tea, then mount high over the Himalayan mountains and as close to the sun as she could. And when the water boiled, she put the tea in, and flew back down over China, out over the ocean, until land came across the horizon again, and she steered her hopes down through the streets of the city and in her front door, just as the tea was perfectly ready.

She poured two cups, and two bowls of cereal,
and took the tray into her parents' bedroom.

"You've sure been busy this morning," said her father.

"I'll say," said Katelyn.

"And I sure hope you've made a big pot of tea,"
said her mother. "I think I just might need it today."

"And I think," said Katelyn, "you might just have enough."

© 2000 Pete Marlowe (text)
© 2000 Charles Bell (illustrations)
Designed by iCheung Design

Annick Press Ltd.

We acknowledge the support of the Canada Council for the Arts, the Ontario Arts Council, and the Government of Canada through the Book Publishing Industry Development Program (BPIDP) for our publishing activities.

Cataloging in Publication Data

Marlowe, Pete
One Arabian Morning

ISBN 1-55037-659-4 (bound)   ISBN 1-55037-658-6)pbk.)

I. Bell, Charles (Charles Stephen). II. Title.

PS8576.A741750S3 2000   jC813'.54   C00-930899-7
PZ7.M37O53 2000

The art in this book was rendered digitally
The text was typeset in Phaistos and Bernhard Modern

visit us at: www.annickpress.com

Distributed in Canada by
Firefly Books Ltd.
3680 Victoria Park Avenue
Willowdale, ON
M2H 3K1

Published in the U.S.A. by
Annick Press (U.S.) Ltd.

Distributed in the U.S.A. by
Firefly Books (U.S.) Inc.
P.O. Box 1338
Ellicott Station
Buffalo, NY 14205

Printed and bound in Canada by
Friesens, Altona, Manitoba.